MARY HAD A LITTLE LAMB

ROCK-A-BYE, BABY

OLD KING

HUMPTY DUMPTY

MOTHER GOOSE

TO MARKET

BAA, BAA,

BLACK SHEEP

LITTLE BOY BLUE

MARY, MARY,

QUITE CONTRARY

LITTLE MISS MUFFET

THE COW JUMPED OVER THE MOON

LADYBIRD BOOKS, INC.
Lewiston, Maine 04240 U.S.A.
© LADYBIRD BOOKS LTD MCMLXXXVII
Loughborough, Leicestershire, England

Printed in England

MOTHER GOOSE

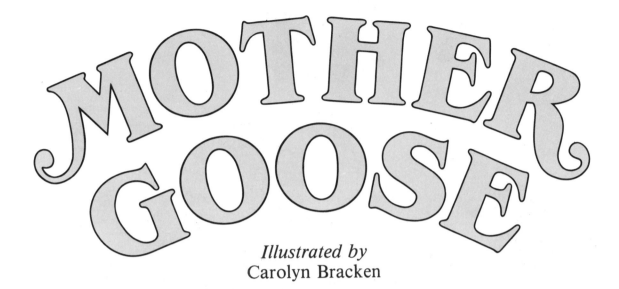

Illustrated by
Carolyn Bracken

Ladybird Books

Cackle, cackle, Mother Goose,
Have you any feathers loose?
Truly have I, pretty fellow,
Half enough to fill a pillow.
Here are quills, take one or two,
And down to make a bed for you.

Baa, baa, black sheep,
    Have you any wool?
Yes, sir, yes, sir,
    Three bags full;
One for the master,
    And one for the dame,
And one for the little boy
    Who lives down the lane.

Little Boy Blue, come blow your horn,
The sheep's in the meadow, the cow's in the corn.
Where is the boy who looks after the sheep?
He's under the haystack, fast asleep.
Will you wake him? No, not I!
For if I do, he's sure to cry.

Little Bo-peep
Has lost her sheep,
And doesn't know where to find them.
Leave them alone,
And they'll come home,
Bringing their tails behind them.

Girls and boys, come out to play,
The moon does shine as bright as day.
Leave your supper, and leave your sleep,
And come with your playfellows into the street.
Come with a whoop, and come with a call,
Come with a good will, or come not at all.
Come let us dance on the open green,
And she who holds longest shall be our queen.

My mother said that I never should
Play with the gypsies in the wood.
The wood was dark; the grass was green;
In came Sally with a tambourine.

Here we go round the mulberry bush,
   The mulberry bush, the mulberry bush,
Here we go round the mulberry bush,
   On a cold and frosty morning!

This is the way we wash our clothes,
   Wash our clothes, wash our clothes,
This is the way we wash our clothes,
   On a cold and frosty morning!

Ring around the rosy,
A pocket full of posies.
   A-tishoo! A-tishoo!
We all fall down.

Jack and Jill went up the hill,
To fetch a pail of water;
Jack fell down, and broke his crown,
And Jill came tumbling after.

Humpty Dumpty sat on a wall,
Humpty Dumpty had a great fall;
All the king's horses,
And all the king's men,
Couldn't put Humpty together again.

The Lion and the Unicorn
   Were fighting for the crown;
The Lion beat the Unicorn
   All around the town.

TOWN

Some gave them white bread,
   And some gave them brown;
Some gave them plum cake,
   And drummed them out of town.

Old King Cole was a merry old soul,
And a merry old soul was he;
He called for his pipe,
And he called for his bowl,
And he called for his fiddlers three.

Sing a song of sixpence,
A pocket full of rye;
Four and twenty blackbirds,
Baked in a pie.

When the pie was opened,
The birds began to sing;
Wasn't that a dainty dish
To set before the king?

The king was in the counting house,
Counting out his money;
The queen was in the parlor,
Eating bread and honey.

The maid was in the garden,
Hanging out the clothes,
When down came a blackbird,
And snipped off her nose!

The Queen of Hearts she made some tarts,
    All on a summer's day;
The Knave of Hearts he stole those tarts,
    And took them clean away.
The King of Hearts called for the tarts,
    And beat the Knave full sore;
The Knave of Hearts brought back the tarts,
    And vowed he'd steal no more.

Pat-a-cake, pat-a-cake, baker's man,
Bake me a cake as fast as you can;
Pat it and prick it, and mark it with B,
And put it in the oven for Baby and me.

Baby and I
Were baked in a pie,
The gravy was wonderful hot.
We had nothing to pay
To the baker that day,
And so we crept out of the pot.

Nose, nose, jolly red nose,
What gave you that jolly red nose?
Nutmeg and ginger, cinnamon and cloves,
That's what gave me this jolly red nose.

Little Jack Horner
Sat in the corner,
Eating a Christmas pie.
He put in his thumb,
And pulled out a plum,
And said, "What a good boy am I!"

Little Miss Muffet
Sat on a tuffet,
Eating her curds and whey.
Along came a spider,
Who sat down beside her,
And frightened Miss Muffet away.

Molly, my sister, and I fell out,
And what do you think it was all about?

She loved coffee and I loved tea,
And that was the reason we could not agree.

Polly, put the kettle on,
Polly, put the kettle on,
Polly, put the kettle on,
    We'll all have tea.

Sukey, take it off again,
Sukey, take it off again,
Sukey, take it off again,
    They've all gone away.

Blow the fire and make the toast,
Put the muffins on to roast,
Who is going to eat the most?
    We'll all have tea.

Andy Pandy, fine and dandy,
Loves plum cake and sugar candy.
Bought it from a candy shop,
And away did hop, hop, hop.

Jack Sprat could eat no fat,
His wife could eat no lean,
And so between them both, you see,
They licked the platter clean.

Peter, Peter, pumpkin eater,
Had a wife and couldn't keep her;
He put her in a pumpkin shell,
And there he kept her very well.

Peter, Peter, pumpkin eater,
Had another, and didn't love her;
Peter learned to read and spell,
And then he loved her very well.

Mary had a little lamb,
    Its fleece was white as snow;
And everywhere that Mary went,
    The lamb was sure to go.

It followed her to school one day,
    That was against the rule;
It made the children laugh and play
    To see a lamb at school.

And so the teacher turned it out,
    But still it lingered near;
And waited patiently about,
    Till Mary did appear.

"Why does the lamb love Mary so?"
    The eager children cry;
"Why, Mary loves the lamb, you know,"
    The teacher did reply.

ABCDEFGHIJKLMNOPQRSTUVWXYZ

A diller, a dollar,
A ten o'clock scholar,
What makes you come so soon?
You used to come at ten o'clock,
But now you come at noon.

ABCDEFGHIJKLMNOPQRSTUVWXYZ

Elsie Marley is grown so fine,
She won't get up to feed the swine,
But lies in bed till eight or nine;
Lazy Elsie Marley.

Hickory, dickory, dock,
The mouse ran up the clock.
The clock struck one,
The mouse ran down,
Hickory, dickory, dock.

Three blind mice, see how they run!
They all ran after the farmer's wife,
Who cut off their tails with a carving knife.
Did you ever see such a sight in your life,
As three blind mice?

Little Robin Redbreast
Sat upon a rail;
Niddle noddle went his head,
Wiggle waggle went his tail.

The north wind doth blow,
And we shall have snow,
And what will poor robin do then,
Poor thing?

He'll sit in a barn,
And keep himself warm,
And hide his head under his wing,
Poor thing.

Blow, wind, blow! And go, mill, go!
That the miller may grind his corn;
That the baker may take it,
And into bread make it,
And bring us a loaf in the morn.

Old Mother Hubbard went to the cupboard
To fetch her poor dog a bone.
But when she got there, the cupboard was bare,
And so the poor dog had none.

There was an old woman lived under a hill,
And if she isn't gone, she lives there still.
Baked apples she sold, and cranberry pies,
And she's the old woman who never told lies.

There was an old woman who lived in a shoe,
She had so many children she didn't know what to do.
She gave them some broth without any bread,
And scolded them soundly and sent them to bed.

When I was a little boy,
I washed my mother's dishes;
Now I am a great big boy,
I roll in golden riches.

When I was a little boy,
I washed my mother's floor;
Now I am a man of wealth,
And drive a coach and four.

Little Tommy Tucker
    Sings for his supper;
What shall we give him?
    White bread and butter.
How shall he cut it
    Without a knife?
How will he be married
    Without a wife?

Curly locks, curly locks, wilt thou be mine?
Thou shalt not wash dishes, nor yet feed the swine;
But sit on a cushion and sew a fine seam,
And feed upon strawberries, sugar, and cream.

Lavender's blue, diddle, diddle,
　　Lavender's green;
When I am king, diddle, diddle,
　　You shall be queen.

On Saturday night shall be my care
To powder my locks and curl my hair;
On Sunday morning my love will come in,
When he will marry me with a gold ring.

Bobby Shaftoe's gone to sea,
Silver buckles on his knee;
He'll come back and marry me,
Bonny Bobby Shaftoe!

Bobby Shaftoe's bright and fair,
Combing down his yellow hair;
He's my love forevermore,
Bonny Bobby Shaftoe!

I saw three ships come sailing by,
    Come sailing by, come sailing by,
I saw three ships come sailing by,
    On New Year's day in the morning.

And what do you think was in them then,
    Was in them then, was in them then?
And what do you think was in them then,
    On New Year's day in the morning?

Three pretty girls were in them then,
    Were in them then, were in them then,
Three pretty girls were in them then,
    On New Year's day in the morning.

One could whistle, and one could sing,
    And one could play the violin;
Such joy there was at my wedding,
    On New Year's day in the morning.

Dance to your daddy,
My little laddie,
Dance to your daddy, my little lamb!
You shall have a fishy
In a little dishy,
You shall have a fishy,
When the boat comes in.

Dance to your daddy,
My little laddie,
Dance to your daddy, my little lamb!
You shall have an apple,
You shall have a plum,
You shall have a rattle-basket,
When your dad comes home.

I saw a ship a-sailing,
      A-sailing on the sea,
And oh, but it was laden
      With pretty things for thee!

There were comfits in the cabin,
      And apples in the hold;
The sails were made of silk,
      And the masts were all of gold.

The four and twenty sailors
      That stood between the decks,
Were four and twenty white mice
      With chains about their necks.

The captain was a duck
      With a packet on his back,
And when the ship began to move,
      The captain said, "Quack! Quack!"

I had a little nut tree,
  Nothing would it bear
But a silver nutmeg
  And a golden pear.
The king of Spain's daughter
  Came to visit me,
And all for the sake
  Of my little nut tree.

Daffy-down-dilly is now come to town,
In a yellow petticoat, and a green gown.

Mary, Mary, quite contrary,
How does your garden grow?
With silver bells and cockle shells,
And pretty maids all in a row.

Pretty maid, pretty maid,
Where have you been?
Gathering roses
To give to the queen.
Pretty maid, pretty maid,
What gave she you?
She gave me a diamond
As big as my shoe.

As I was going to St. Ives,
I met a man with seven wives.
Each wife had seven sacks,
Each sack had seven cats,
Each cat had seven kits.
Kits, cats, sacks, and wives,
How many were going to St. Ives?

(Answer: Only one – "I")

Simple Simon met a pieman
    Going to the fair;
Said Simple Simon to the pieman,
    "Let me taste your ware."

Said the pieman to Simple Simon,
    "Show me first your penny."
Said Simple Simon to the pieman,
    "Indeed, I have not any."

Oh, dear, what can the matter be?
Dear, dear, what can the matter be?
Oh, dear, what can the matter be?
Johnny's so long at the fair.

He promised to buy me a pair of sleeve buttons,
A pair of new garters that cost him but tuppence;
He promised he'd bring me a bunch of blue ribbons
To tie up my bonny brown hair.

One misty, moisty morning,
When cloudy was the weather,
There I met an old man
Clothed all in leather;
Clothed all in leather,
With cap under his chin.
How do you do, and how do you do,
And how do you do again?

Hark, hark, the dogs do bark,
The beggars are coming to town;
Some in rags, and some in jags,
And some in velvet gowns.

If I'd as much money as I could spend,
I never would cry old chairs to mend,
Old chairs to mend, old chairs to mend,
I never would cry old chairs to mend.

If I'd as much money as I could tell,
I never would cry old clothes to sell,
Old clothes to sell, old clothes to sell,
I never would cry old clothes to sell.

See-saw, Margery Daw,
Jacky shall have a new master;
Jacky shall have but a penny a day,
Because he can't work any faster.

Ride a cock-horse to Banbury Cross,
To see a fine lady upon a white horse;
Rings on her fingers, and bells on her toes,
And she shall have music wherever she goes.

Yankee Doodle went to town,
    Riding on a pony;
He stuck a feather in his cap,
    And called it macaroni.

I had a little pony,
    His name was Dapple Gray;
I lent him to a lady,
    To ride a mile away.
She whipped him, she slashed him,
    She rode him through the mire;
I would not lend my pony now,
    For all the lady's hire.

It's raining, it's pouring,
The old man is snoring;
He went to bed,
And bumped his head,
And couldn't get up in the morning.

Doctor Foster went to Gloucester
In a shower of rain;
He stepped in a puddle,
Right up to his middle,
And never went there again.

Rain on the green grass,
And rain on the tree;
Rain on the house-top,
But not on me.

Barber, barber, shave a pig,
How many hairs to make a wig?
Four and twenty, that's enough,
Give the barber a pinch of snuff.

To market, to market, to buy a fat pig,
Home again, home again, jiggety jig.
To market, to market, to buy a fat hog,
Home again, home again, jiggety jog.

This little piggy went to market,

This little piggy stayed home.

This little piggy had roast beef,

This little piggy had none.

And this little piggy said, "Wee, wee, wee," all the way home.

Dickery, dickery, dare,
The pig flew up in the air;
The man in brown
Soon brought him down,
Dickery, dickery, dare.

Peter Piper picked a peck of pickled peppers;
Did Peter Piper pick a peck of pickled peppers?

If Peter Piper picked a peck of pickled peppers,
Where's the peck of pickled peppers Peter Piper picked?

Up and down the City Road,
    In and out the Eagle,
That's the way the money goes,
    Pop goes the weasel!

Half a pound of tuppenny rice,
    Half a pound of treacle,
Mix it up and make it nice,
    Pop goes the weasel!

Pease porridge hot, pease porridge cold,
Pease porridge in the pot, nine days old.

Some like it hot, some like it cold,
Some like it in the pot, nine days old.

One, two, buckle my shoe;   Three, four, open the door;   Five, six, pick up sticks;

Seven, eight, lay them straight;   Nine, ten, a big fat hen;

Eleven, twelve, dig and delve;   Thirteen, fourteen,
maids a-courting;   Fifteen, sixteen,
maids in the kitchen;

Seventeen, eighteen,
maids in waiting;   Nineteen, twenty, my plate's empty.

Hickety, pickety, my black hen,
She lays eggs for gentlemen;
Gentlemen come every day,
To see what my black hen doth lay.
Sometimes nine and sometimes ten,
She lays eggs for gentlemen.

One, two, three, four, five,
Once I caught a fish alive.
Why did you let it go?
Because it bit my finger so.

Six, seven, eight, nine, ten,
Shall we go to fish again?
Not today, some other time,
For I have broke my fishing line.

When I was a little girl,
    About seven years old,
I hadn't got a petticoat,
    To keep me from the cold.

So I went to Darlington,
    That pretty little town,
And there I bought a petticoat,
    A cloak, and a gown.

Lucy Locket lost her pocket,
Kitty Fisher found it;
Not a penny was there in it,
Only ribbon round it.

Little Betty Blue
Lost her holiday shoe,
What can little Betty do?
Give her another,
To match the other,
And then she may walk out in two.

Cobbler, Cobbler, mend my shoe,
Get it done by half-past two;
Stitch it up, and stitch it down,
Then I'll give you half a crown.

Goosey, goosey, gander,
   Whither shall I wander?
Upstairs, downstairs,
   In my lady's chamber.

Pussy cat, pussy cat, where have you been?
I've been to London to look at the queen.
Pussy cat, pussy cat, what did you there?
I frightened a little mouse under her chair.

Six little mice sat down to spin;
Pussy passed by, and she peeped in.
What are you doing, my little men?
Weaving coats for gentlemen.
Shall I come in and cut off your threads?
No, no, Mistress Pussy, you'd bite off our heads.
Oh, no, I won't, I'll help you spin.
That may be so, but you can't come in.

Pussy Cat Mole jumped over a coal,
And in her best petticoat burnt a great hole.
Pussy Cat Mole shall have no more milk,
Until her best petticoat's mended with silk.

Here am I,
Little Jumping Joan;
When nobody's with me,
I'm all alone.

Jack, be nimble,
Jack, be quick,
Jack, jump over the candlestick.

Rub-a-dub-dub,
Three men in a tub,
And who do you think they be?
The butcher, the baker,
The candlestick-maker;
Turn 'em out, knaves all three.

How many miles to Babylon?
Three score miles and ten.
Can I get there by candlelight?
Yes, and back again.
If your heels are nimble and light,
You may get there by candlelight.

There was a crooked man,
And he walked a crooked mile,
He found a crooked sixpence
Against a crooked stile;
He bought a crooked cat,
Which caught a crooked mouse,
And they all lived together,
In a crooked little house.

Tweedledum and Tweedledee
    Agreed to fight a battle,
For Tweedledum said Tweedledee
    Had spoiled his nice new rattle.
Just then flew by a monstrous crow,
    As black as a tar barrel,
Which frightened both the heroes so,
    They quite forgot their battle.

Georgie Porgie, pudding and pie,
Kissed the girls and made them cry;
When the boys came out to play,
Georgie Porgie ran away.

Ding, dong, bell, pussy's in the well.
Who put her in? Little Johnny Green.
Who pulled her out? Little Tommy Stout.
What a naughty boy was that,
To try to drown poor pussy cat,
Who never did any harm,
But killed the mice in his father's barn.

I love little pussy,
    Her coat is so warm,
And if I don't hurt her,
    She'll do me no harm.
So I'll not pull her tail,
    Nor drive her away,
But pussy and I
    Very gently will play.

A cat came fiddling out of a barn,
With a pair of bagpipes under her arm;
She could sing nothing but "Fiddle-de-dee,
The mouse has married the bumblebee."
Pipe, cat; dance, mouse;
We'll have a wedding at our good house.

Cock-a-doodle-doo!
My dame has lost her shoe,
My master's lost his fiddling stick,
And knows not what to do.

Cock-a-doodle-doo!
What is my dame to do?
Till master finds his fiddling stick,
She'll dance without her shoe.

Cock-a-doodle-doo!
My dame has found her shoe,
And master's found his fiddling stick,
Sing doodle-doodle-doo.

Cock-a-doodle-doo!
My dame will dance with you,
While master fiddles his fiddling stick
For dame and doodle-doo.

Hey diddle diddle,
The cat and the fiddle,
The cow jumped over the moon;
The little dog laughed
To see such sport,
And the dish ran away with the spoon.

Sally go round the sun,
Sally go round the moon,
Sally go round the chimney-pots
On a Saturday afternoon.

There was an old woman tossed up in a basket,
    Seventeen times as high as the moon;
And where she was going, I couldn't but ask it,
    For under her arm she carried a broom.
Old woman, old woman, old woman, said I,
    Whither, oh whither, oh whither so high?
To sweep the cobwebs from the sky!
    Shall I go with you? Aye, by and by.

What's the news of the day,
Good neighbor, I pray?
They say a balloon
Is gone up to the moon!

I see the moon,
And the moon sees me.
God bless the moon,
And God bless me.

Wee Willie Winkie runs through the town,
Upstairs and downstairs, in his nightgown,
Rapping at the window, crying through the lock,
"Are the children all in bed,
For now it's eight o'clock?"

Diddle diddle dumpling, my son John,
Went to bed with his trousers on;
One shoe off, and one shoe on,
Diddle diddle dumpling, my son John.

Rock-a-bye, baby, in the tree top,
When the wind blows, the cradle will rock;
When the bough breaks, the cradle will fall;
Down will come baby, cradle, and all.

Hush, little baby, don't say a word,

Papa's going to buy you a mockingbird.
If that mockingbird won't sing,

Papa's going to buy you a diamond ring.
If that diamond ring turns brass,

Papa's going to buy you a looking-glass.
If that looking-glass gets broke,

Papa's going to buy you a billy goat.
If that billy goat won't pull,

Papa's going to buy you a cart and bull.
If that cart and bull fall down,

You'll still be the sweetest little baby in town!

Star light, star bright,
First star I see tonight,
I wish I may, I wish I might,
Have the wish I wish tonight.

Good night,
Sleep tight,
Wake up bright
In the morning light,
To do what's right
With all your might.